For you are fearfully and
wonderfully made.

PSALM 139

For Harry, Eleanor, Olivia, Jonathan, and Emily—I'm so glad you came! —SLJ

For Florence L., who first introduced me to quokkas. —ET

Requests for information should be addressed to:
Zonderkidz, 3900 Sparks Drive SE, Grand Rapids, Michigan 49546

Art direction & design: Brooke Reynolds for inchmark

Printed in Korea

22 23 24 25 26 /SAM/ 6 5 4 3 2 1

Little One,
We Knew You'd Come

written by Sally Lloyd-Jones

illustrated by Eve Tharlet

Little one, we knew you'd come.

We hoped.

We dreamed.

We watched for you.

We counted the days till you were due.

We waited. How we longed for you,

And the day that you were born.

Little one, we knew you'd come.

It was late at night. The time had come.

The time for you to come, my love.

You'll be here soon. We're ready for you,

And the day that you were born.

Little one, we knew you'd come.

By silver stars and golden moon,

At break of dawn, you came.

Kiss your nose, those tiny toes,

On the day that you were born.

Little one, we knew you'd come.

People were sleeping. We didn't care.

Good news, we sang, our baby is here!

Our baby has come, our darling one,

Oh, the day that you were born.

Little one, we knew you'd come.

Kiss and cuddle and love the baby.

Scoop that beautiful baby up.

And sing a soft, sweet lullaby,

On the day that you were born.

Little one, we knew you'd come.

And every year, we remember you,

Our miracle child, our dreams come true.

Oh, how we thank God for you,

And the day that you were born.

Little one ...

... we're so glad you've come!